This ʰ

THIS WALKER BOOK BELONGS TO:

_____

_____

_____

_____

*For Rosie*

First published 1992 by Walker Books Ltd
87 Vauxhall Walk
London SE11 5HJ

2 4 6 8 10 9 7 5 3

© 1992 Catherine and Laurence Anholt

Printed in Hong Kong

British Library Cataloguing in Publication Data
A catalogue record for this book is available from the British Library

ISBN 0-7445-3011-3

# KIDS

*Catherine and Laurence Anholt*

WALKER BOOKS
LONDON

# We are the kids!

Big kids, small kids, tiny kids, tall kids

Happy kids, grumpy kids, skinny kids, dumpy kids

# Look out, here we come!

Slow kids, quick kids, healthy kids, sick kids

Smooth kids, hairy kids, cute kids, scary kids

# What are kids like?

Kids are silly, kids are funny,

Kids have noses that are runny.

Some kids wash but some are smelly,

Both kinds like to watch the telly.

# What do kids look like?

Freckles and badges and ink on their skirts,

Glasses and smiles and hanging-out shirts.

Kids put their left foot
where the right one should be,

They have gaps in their teeth
and a cut on each knee.

# What do kids do?

mix

mess

muddle

comfort

kiss

cuddle

laugh

leap

lick

poke

push

pick

scratch

scream

scrawl

break

bellow

bawl

# Where do kids hide?

Seven in a bed, six in a box,

Five behind curtains, four behind clocks,

Three up a tree, two down a hole.

Here is a kid who hid in some coal.

# What's in a kid's pocket?

rubber band

stones and sand

handkerchief

pretty leaf

jam and bread

someone's head

bits of string

another thing

# What do kids make?

Houses with blankets,

Mountains on stairs,

Seas out of carpets,

Trains out of chairs.

# What scares kids?

A slithering snake and a slippery slug,
A girl-eating ghoul and a boy-biting bug,

A gremlin, a goblin, a ghost in the dark,
A tiny black spider, a giant white shark.

# What are kids' secrets?

A ladybird in a
matchbox,

A letter under
a bed,

A horrid pie in a horrible place,

A den behind a shed.

# What are nasty kids like?

They pull your hair, they call you names,
They tell you lies, they spoil your games,
They draw on walls, scream on the floor.
Nasty kids want more, more, more.

# What are nice kids like?

They make you laugh, they hold your hand,
Nice kids always understand.
They share their toys, they let you play,
They chase the nasty kids away.

# What do kids dream of?

A ladder to the moon,

A candy tree in bloom,

Riding a flying fish,

Having anything they wish.

# What do mums and dads do?

Tidy, carry, clean and cook,

Bath the baby, read a book, then...

Kiss us when
It's nearly night:
Dads and mums
Switch off the light.

# MORE WALKER PAPERBACKS
## For You to Enjoy

### Also by Catherine and Laurence Anholt

### WHAT I LIKE

"Children's likes and dislikes, as seen by six children but with a universality which makes them appealing to all... The scant, rhyming text is elegantly fleshed out by delicate illustrations full of tiny details." *Children's Books of the Year*

0-7445-3019-9   £3.99

### HERE COME THE BABIES

"Over 70 warm and funny pictures of babies to amuse and entertain – especially those with a younger brother or sister... This jolly book is sure to be popular from babyhood right up until first reading skills are acquired."
*Practical Parenting*

0-7445-3617-0   £3.99

### THE TWINS, TWO BY TWO

"All families will be able to relate to this super book about bedtime... An irresistible end-of-the-day story just right for reading together." *Practical Parenting*

0-7445-3142-X   £3.99

**Walker Paperbacks are available from most booksellers, or by post from Walker Books Ltd, PO Box 11, Falmouth, Cornwall TR10 9EN.**

To order, send: Title, author, ISBN number and price for each book ordered, your full name and address, cheque or postal order for the total amount, plus postage and packing:

UK and BFPO Customers – £1.00 for first book, plus 50p for the second book and plus 30p for each additional book to a maximum charge of £3.00.
Overseas and Eire Customers – £2.00 for first book, plus £1.00 for the second book and plus 50p per copy for each additional book.
Prices are correct at time of going to press, but are subject to change without notice.